Of All Places to

Park Addams was in the boys' bathroom minding his own business when it happened.

He was in a hurry. The bell was about to ring. He wasn't even thinking about what Alex said had happened to him in the bathroom the day before.

He charged in and checked out the stalls. A pair of feet in red sneakers was under the first stall door. No problem. He went into the other stall.

He closed the door.

Then he realized what he'd seen in the stall next to him.

Park shut his eyes. A chill crept up his back. Slowly he opened his eyes. Slowly he bent down to peer under the wall that divided the two bathroom stalls.

The red sneakers were still there. They were half hidden behind a giant spiderweb. As Park watched, a shiny black spider dropped down and then climbed back up.

That was unsettling. But not really frightening. It wasn't the spider that made Park's mouth drop open and his eyes bulge out.

It was the shoes. And the socks. As Park watched, one of the toes of the shoes began to tap slowly.

Tap. Tap. Tap.

But there were no legs coming out of the shoes. Above the socks, which seemed to be standing up of their own accord, was nothing but thin air. . . .

Other Skylark Books you won't want to miss!

SPELL IT M-U-R-D-E-R *by Ivy Ruckman*
PRONOUNCE IT DEAD *by Ivy Ruckman*
THE GHOST WORE GRAY *by Bruce Coville*
THE GHOST IN THE BIG BRASS BED *by Bruce Coville*
THE GHOST IN THE THIRD ROW *by Bruce Coville*
ELVIS IS BACK, AND HE'S IN THE SIXTH GRADE!
by Stephen Mooser
THEY'RE TORTURING TEACHERS IN ROOM 104
by Jerry Piasecki
WHAT IS THE TEACHER'S TOUPEE DOING
IN THE FISH TANK? *by Jerry Piasecki*

GRAVEYARD SCHOOL

There's a Ghost in the Boys' Bathroom

Tom B. Stone

A SKYLARK BOOK

Toronto New York London Sydney Auckland

RL 3.1, 008–012

THERE'S A GHOST IN THE BOYS' BATHROOM
A Skylark Book / January 1996

GRAVEYARD SCHOOL

There's a Ghost in the Boys' Bathroom

CHAPTER
1

He was in the boys' bathroom minding his own business when he smelled it.

He sniffed.

He made a face.

It was disgusting. Terrible. A nose bomb. It was the worst smell Alex Lee had ever smelled. Worse than the school lunchroom. Worse than the bottom of a locker at the end of the year. Worse than anything he had ever smelled in or out of the bathroom.

Alex sniffed again. What did it smell like? Smoke? Sort of. But what else? Nothing familiar. He couldn't imagine what would cause a smell like that.

He decided not to wait around to find out.

He threw open the stall door. The boys' bathroom on the first floor of the school, the one in the back, closest to the old graveyard, looked the way it always did. No wall of putrid smoke hanging in the air. Nothing disgusting oozing out from under the other stall doors.

The bathroom was empty. Just him and a couple of stalls, a row of urinals, three sinks, and the usual overflowing garbage can. No different from any of the other boys' bathrooms in the school, except that this was the newest and therefore the cleanest. The paint was an ugly green, but not yet gross. The opaque windows overlooking the graveyard weren't quite as grimy as in the other bathrooms. Weak light shined through the glass.

Nothing else. The bathroom was empty.

For a moment Alex thought he'd been imagining things—until he took another deep breath.

"Gag me," he muttered. He grabbed his nose with his fingers and shot across the bathroom. He almost knocked over Bentley Jeste and Tyson Walker as he barreled out the door.

"Hey! Get a grip!" complained Tyson, dodging neatly to one side. Tyson was a star on the boys' soccer team at Graveyard School, so he was quick on his feet.

Ignoring Tyson, Alex grabbed Bent's sleeve. Bent was famous—or infamous—as the practical-joke king of the school. Still holding his nose with his free hand, Alex demanded, " 'Ow'd 'ou oo it, 'ent?"

"Do what?" said Bent. "And why are you talking through your nose?"

Alex let go of his nose. He sniffed the air cautiously. The smell was basic Graveyard School hallway, nothing more. Not his or any kid's favorite smell, maybe, but not life-threatening.

Not like the bathroom.

"How did you do it?" Alex repeated. "How did you make the bathroom smell like that?"

Bent grinned his wicked grin. "Nose bomb, huh? *I* didn't have anything to do with it, Alex." He gave Alex a significant look.

"It—it wasn't me . . . ," Alex began to sputter.

Park Addams came out of a nearby classroom, looked in their direction, and walked toward them.

"Hey," he said. "What's happening?"

Bent grinned more widely. "Alex thinks the bathroom smells funny."

Park, Bent, and Tyson all began to laugh.

"It's not funny," said Alex, getting annoyed. "Check it out." He threw open the bathroom door and motioned the three of them in.

Tyson went in first. And reeled back. He shook his short dreadlocks and blinked his brown eyes rapidly and swallowed hard. "Whoa," he said. "That's . . . that's . . ."

"Outrageous!" exclaimed Park, backing out of the bathroom so quickly that the door slammed behind him. It flew open again instantly and Bent popped out like a

3

jack-in-the-box. His sharp blue eyes were watering from the overpowering aroma. "It smells like something *died* in there," he said.

"It smells like *lots* of things died in there," said Alex.

"Something's probably blocked," said Park, not sounding entirely displeased. "We should tell Basement Bart."

That suggestion brought the conversation to a halt. Then Tyson said, "Well, you're the one who discovered the smell, Alex. You tell him."

"That's not fair," protested Alex.

"Or you could tell Dr. Morthouse," offered Bentley.

"You want me to go the principal and tell her the boys' bathroom stinks?" Alex said. "No way . . . and I'm not going down to the basement to find Basement Bart, either."

Everyone stared at him. He stared back defiantly. Finally Tyson said, "Why? Are you chicken?"

Bent made a clucking sound.

Alex folded his arms and glared. "No, I'm not chicken. I'm just smart. And I'm too young to die."

They all considered that for a moment. Then Park said, "I've never heard that Basement Bart killed a kid, or anything."

"I've never heard that he hasn't," retorted Alex, only half kidding.

Basement Bart was the school janitor. He was big. Surly. Unfriendly. He wore camouflage pants and shirts and he kept his hair tied in a ponytail. He always wore dark glasses. Very dark glasses.

No one knew where he came from. No one knew where he lived. No one ever saw him entering or leaving the school. He was just there. Weirdly there.

Basement Bart was just one of the reasons that Grove Hill Elementary School, situated at one edge of the town of Grove Hill, was called Graveyard School by all its students. Another reason was the old, abandoned (and, some said, haunted) graveyard on the hill behind the school. But most of all, the school had earned—and kept—its nickname because of all the strange, freaky, and frightening things that kept happening around it. Things that the adults, of course, never seemed to notice.

Or worse, things that the adults seemed to believe had perfectly normal explanations.

But in the world of Graveyard School, nothing was normal. Alex sometimes wondered if the rest of the world was any different. He hadn't heard anything particularly horrifying about the junior high school. Or the high school. But maybe by the time all the kids got there from Graveyard School, horrible things just seemed ordinary. Not worth commenting on.

The warning bell rang. Time to get to the next class.

Everyone looked at Alex.

"Hey! I have to get to class!" said Alex. "Besides, the smell is probably going away by now anyway."

"What if it isn't?" said Bent. "What if some unsuspecting little kid opens the door and walks in and is over-whelmed? He passes out, falls on the floor and . . ." Bent clutched his throat and bugged his eyes out. "No more little kid. That'd be all your fault."

"Would not," said Alex automatically.

"Would too."

"No way," said Alex. But what if Bent was right?

Alex had a vision of a tiny little first-grade shape with tiny little first-grader shoes being carried out of the boys' bathroom. People were crying. They were pointing at Alex. "He did it," someone said. "Coward," someone else whispered.

Then Alex remembered that Mr. Dovitch was his teacher for the next class. "I'll tell Mr. Dovitch," said Alex. "He's cool. He'll know what to do."

"Excellent," said Park, and began to lead the way down the hall.

Bent looked disappointed.

Tyson grinned knowingly. "Good save," he said.

Alex grinned back. "Yeah," he said. He didn't even like to think about how close he'd come to having to go in search of Basement Bart—maybe even down into the dark, dark basement that gave the janitor his name. He had an office down there.

Although no one had ever seen it.

"Yeah," Alex said again as he reached the classroom door. "No problem."

6

CHAPTER
2

"Alex? Have you got a problem with that?'' asked Mr. Dovitch.

Alex could feel the eyes of the whole class on his back. He was standing at the front of the room by Mr. Dovitch's desk, where he'd stopped on the way to his desk to report the smell in the boys' bathroom.

Mr. Dovitch had said, "Really? Hmmm. Sounds like a job for Mr. Bartholomew." Then, to Alex's horror, Mr. Dovitch had said, "Wait." He'd scribbled something on a piece of paper, folded it in half, and handed it, along with a hall pass, to Alex. "Go find Mr. Bartholomew and give him the note. He'll take care of it."

Shocked, Alex had looked down at the note and then back into Mr. Dovitch's mild gray eyes. He'd always thought Mr. Dovitch was a relatively nice teacher, especially for Graveyard School. Who knew he had such hidden depths of meanness.

"B-But . . . ," Alex had stammered. Of course he had a problem with it. Only it wasn't a problem he could tell Mr. Dovitch.

"No," he said finally through stiff lips. "No, no problem."

Then it got worse. Mr. Dovitch looked at his watch. "He's probably on break right now. Check his office in the basement first, okay, Alex?"

"What!" Alex had yelped in spite of himself.

Mr. Dovitch frowned.

"I mean, I don't know where his office is," Alex said. "I mean, maybe someone else—"

"You know where the door to the basement is. Mr. Bartholomew's office is in the basement, just to the right of the stairs."

Alex couldn't think of anything else to say. He nodded numbly. Then he walked slowly toward the door to meet his doom.

As Alex reached the door, Mr. Dovitch said, "And I don't need to remind you not to dawdle, do I?"

"No," said Alex. And thought, *I wonder if disappearing counts as dawdling. I wonder how long it will be before they send a search party when I don't come back.*

The door of the basement groaned heavily open.

Far, far below, down a shadowy flight of stone steps, a dim light shined. Alex cleared his throat. "Mr. Bartholomew!" he called.

There was no echo. Alex's voice disappeared as if something living at the bottom of the stairs had eaten it up.

He tried again. "Mr. Bartholomew. It's, ah . . ." He paused. He didn't really want Basement Bart to know his name. What if the janitor remembered that Alex was the one who, in fourth grade, had thrown up on the front steps after school? What if Basement Bart still hated Alex for that? What if he'd been waiting all this time just to get Alex?

"It's, ah, someone sent by Mr. Dovitch. Mr. Bartholomew?"

The words fell like stones to the bottom of a bottomless well.

He was going to have to go in. He took a deep breath and pushed the door open as wide as he could so that there would be more light. He started down the stairs.

Although the basement was dark and creepy, the stairs didn't creak. Nor did any cobwebs brush against his face.

But he couldn't be sure that something didn't go skittering away in the shadows at his feet as he reached the bottom of the steps.

He flinched, but he managed not to scream. He cleared his throat. "Mr. Bartholomew?"

Silence. But ahead, in the dim light, Alex could see a door. With another deep breath, he walked forward. To his left and right, tunnels of darkness loomed. Did the basement go all the way under Graveyard School? Or maybe even beyond? Maybe one of the tunnels led to the old graveyard. Maybe students had gotten lost and died in a maze of Graveyard School tunnels. It could have been a form of punishment invented by Dr. Morthouse: "Go to the basement at once! And don't come out alive."

Maybe Basement Bart sleeps in one of the graves up on the hill . . .

Alex raised his hand and knocked. The door was thick and heavy. His knuckles barely made a sound.

He peered at the door more closely. The word BARTHOLOMEW had been neatly printed on it in black paint. Below it, in much larger, menacing red letters, were two words: KEEP OUT.

That was fair. Alex could keep out. In fact, he could leave. Right now.

He turned to go and noticed that the door was slightly ajar. He stopped.

Maybe Basement Bart was inside. Maybe he was just

asleep at his desk. Or, if he didn't have a desk, asleep in a chair. He had to have a chair.

Although, come to think of it, Alex had never seen Basement Bart sitting down.

Alex nervously began to fold the note in his hands into smaller and smaller squares. Should he push the door open? Maybe he could just slide the note under it.

He folded the note one more time. He bent over to slide it under the door. As he did, the door groaned slightly and began to open.

Alex froze. Then, still bent over, he slowly raised his head to peer into Basement Bart's office.

But before he could see anything, a hand grabbed the back of his jeans and jerked him up so fast and hard that he almost left his high-tops on the floor.

"Whadya think you're doin', kid?" Basement Bart growled in Alex's ear. He swung Alex around, and Alex found himself eyeball to dark glasses with the janitor.

"Nothing! Nothing!" Alex croaked. He flailed his arms and kicked his feet. But Basement Bart held him effortlessly, as if Alex were a weird dancing mop.

"That's what doin' nothing looks like, eh?" said Basement Bart. "Spying on people, are you?"

"No! Note! I brought you a note!" Alex said, pointing.

Still holding Alex aloft, Basement Bart leaned forward and peered down at the tiny square of white paper on the floor at the edge of the door. He grunted and let Alex go. Alex dropped to the floor on all fours and scrambled to his feet as Basement Bart picked up the note.

The janitor unfolded the note and began to read it. Alex began to back cautiously toward the stairs. But he'd barely reached the bottom step when one of Basement Bart's big, beefy paws shot out and caught him by the shoulder. "A bad smell in the new boys' bathroom."

Alex tried in vain to twist free. "I have to get back to class," he gasped.

If the janitor had heard, he didn't show it. His hand still firmly clamped on Alex's shoulder, he swept Alex up the stairs and into the hall.

When they reached the bathroom, Basement Bart let go. Alex briefly considered making a run for it, but he knew it would be hopeless.

Basement Bart pushed the bathroom door open. He smiled a mirthless smile. "Okay," he said. "Let's take a smell."

They stepped inside.

Alex sniffed. Basement Bart snorted.

"There's nothing wrong with this bathroom," the janitor said in his expressionless, cold voice.

"Yes there is! It stinks. Or it did!"

Basement Bart sniffed. He still didn't change expression. But he seemed to freeze suddenly. He swung his head around.

With a shiver, Alex rubbed the goose bumps that had

suddenly come up on his arms. Although the steam radiator was on in the corner, he was suddenly very, very cold.

"And it's freezing in here," he said, feeling his teeth start to chatter. He half expected to see frost forming on the windows and mirrors.

The janitor didn't answer. He turned his head slowly left and right. Then he said, "Burning smell."

"Yes! That's it!" Alex nodded. "Only . . . worse."

Basement Bart wheeled abruptly and began to walk out of the bathroom.

"Hey!" said Alex. "It doesn't smell like that now. How did you know?"

He started after Basement Bart. He could feel the icy tiles of the floor all the way through the soles of his shoes. He felt as if he were moving in slow motion. Frozen slow motion. Super fro-mo.

"Hey!" he said again. He reached the door, which had just swung shut behind the janitor. His voice sounded thin and faraway.

He pushed on the door. It didn't move.

"Hey! Hey, let me out!" said Alex. He pushed on the door again. It stayed frozen shut.

Frozen shut?

Alex blinked. The entire door was framed in ice. Coated with it.

What's going on here? In a sudden panic, Alex threw himself shoulder first against the door.

A sudden, horrible belching sound erupted behind him. The foul burning odor came back. Alex looked over his shoulder and saw thick, greasy black smoke billowing toward him in a solid wall.

As he watched, long, clawlike hands reached out from the smoke for him.

"No!" Alex cried. "Noooooo!"

CHAPTER
3

Alex pounded on the door. His fists slid off the slippery coat of ice. Although he was shouting, his voice sounded tiny and faraway.

Then, without warning, the door burst open and Alex tumbled out to fall at Basement Bart's feet.

He'd never been so glad to see a big, ugly pair of feet in his life.

The feet moved menacingly in front of Alex's nose, and he jumped up. He pointed with a trembling hand. "Ice . . . ," he gasped. "Smoke. Hands. Claws." He made his hand into a claw.

Basement Bart pushed the bathroom door open and went inside again. Cautiously Alex followed him.

Nothing. No smoke. No ice. But the smell of smoke was there now. Faint. Fetid. Disgusting.

Basement Bart looked over his shoulder. "You been playing with matches in here, kid?"

"No!" Alex prepared to defend himself. "I don't have any matches. I . . ."

But to Alex's surprise, the janitor appeared to take Alex's word. He nodded and went back out again.

Taking no chances, Alex followed Basement Bart so closely that he stepped on his heels as they returned to the hall.

Basement Bart turned. "Back off, kid," he growled.

"Yep. Sorry. Uh . . ." Alex's heart was still pounding. He could still feel the cold, slimy ice under his hands. He could still see the ghastly claws reaching out from the smoke.

Basement Bart waited, his dark glasses focused on Alex.

Alex swallowed hard. "Uh . . . ," he began again. "Do you think something is wrong with the, uh, bathroom?"

With a shrug, Basement Bart said, "Nothing I can fix."

He turned and walked away.

"Wait!" said Alex.

"What?"

"My pass," said Alex. "You have to sign my pass."

Basement Bart reached into his pocket and took out the crumpled hall pass. He extracted a stub of a pencil and made a mark on the pass and held it out.

Alex took it.

Then he took off. Whatever was going on was too weird for words. He'd made it to the end of the hall before Basement Bart's voice stopped him.

"Hey, kid. I'd stay out of that bathroom, if I was you."

Alex turned.

But Basement Bart was nowhere in sight. The hall was empty—except for a faint red glow coming from under the door of the boys' bathroom.

Maria Medina and Stacey Carter walked by holding their lunch trays. Carefully balancing her tray on one hand, Maria grabbed her nose with the other. Stacey did the same. Then the two girls let go of their noses and burst out laughing.

Alex made a face. Park said, "Get a life."

"Oooooh," said Stacey. She and Maria stopped and put their trays down at the other end of the long table.

"Ummmm," said Maria. She sniffed. "Something smells—interesting."

Jaws Bennett, a strongly built kid with an iron stomach who was famous all over school for being able to eat anything, "even roadkill," as he boasted, said, "Lunch."

Jokes about how the school lunches smelled and looked were old news. Nobody laughed. Jaws took a large forkful of an unidentified gray object. " 's 'urkey loaf," he mumbled as he chewed.

Alex rolled his eyes. Jaws's real name was Alexander (although no one except the principal and the assistant principal and Jaws's parents ever called him that), but that was the only thing he and Jaws had in common. Alex couldn't imagine *enjoying* eating the school lunches.

Maria sniffed again. "No. No, it's not lunch I'm talking about." She and Stacey sat down. Maria brushed her dark, spiky bangs back off her forehead so that they stood up. She stared down the table at Alex. Her brown eyes glinted with laughter.

Stacey flipped her own long, brown braid over her shoulder and looked at Alex and grinned.

Alex said, "It's not funny, you know." His brown eyes darkened at the memory of those claws, reaching out from the smoke. He hadn't imagined it. He knew he hadn't.

Then he added hopelessly, "And you didn't have to go and tell everybody, Park."

"Me?" Park looked shocked. Then he raised his voice. "Tyson's the one who's going around the school talking bathrooms."

"Not," said Tyson, who was walking by. He tipped his head and his dreads bounced. "You know who it was."

They all looked at the table toward which Tyson continued to walk. At it sat Bent, school math whiz Jordie Flanders, class president Kirstin Bjorg, and the skateboard rulers of the school, Skate McGraw and Vickie Wheilson.

"Gee, the high-achievement table," said Maria sarcastically.

"Bent," said Alex resignedly. How could he have forgotten that Bent had been there when Alex had first come flying out of the bathroom that morning? Of course Bent had told the whole school by now. Bent loved to tell stories. Especially funny stories. And Alex was sure that Bent had made this story even funnier.

He was just glad he hadn't told Bent what had happened when he'd gone back to the bathroom with Basement Bart.

In fact, he hadn't told anybody. He'd been so shaken up that he'd sat silently at his desk through the rest of his morning classes. But then, he was normally a quiet guy. And Park was more than willing to talk.

The way he was doing now. "It was the smell that ate the school, Alex isn't kidding," he said. "How'dja do it, Alex?"

"I didn't," said Alex. His face turned red as he realized that Stacey and Maria were listening intently. Why did Park have to talk about this in front of the girls?

"Do we have to have this disgusting conversation now?" asked a snotty voice. Perfect Polly Hannah sat down next to Maria. She unfolded her napkin and smoothed it over the lap of her pink jeans.

Polly was the only girl in the school, and possibly in

19

the universe, who owned pink jeans. Pink was Polly's favorite color. Today she was wearing a pink-and-green-striped cotton sweater, a pink headband, pale green socks, and perfectly polished loafers.

A tattletale and a whiner, Polly was universally disliked. But she was so self-assured that she never noticed.

For once, Alex was glad to see her. He said, "Polly's right. We shouldn't talk about this at lunch."

"Flush twice," said Park gleefully. "It's a long way to the lunchroom!"

Polly's cheeks turned pinker than her jeans. She slammed her fork down. "Stop that!" she said. "Stop it right now."

"Round and round and round it goes," chanted Park. "Where it stops, nobody knows."

Alex began to feel a little sick himself. Since he could never admit that, he quickly said, "Has anyone here ever seen inside Basement Bart's office?"

That changed the subject. No one had, of course. In fact, Alex was the only kid who had made it all the way to the door of Basement Bart's office. Stacey had made it to the top of the basement stairs once, in fourth grade, but the janitor had found her and without a word had taken the note she was delivering, then closed the door in her face.

"You're lucky you didn't get lost in the basement," said Polly.

"I bet those tunnels lead all the way to Slime Lake, or something," said Maria.

"Yeah, right," said Park.

"Well, maybe not to Slime Lake," said Maria. "But you know they go back to the old graveyard."

"Has anyone ever seen Basement Bart leave the school?" asked Alex.

No one had.

"He probably sleeps in his office. And lives in the underground tunnels. Like that Greek myth guy. You know, the Minotaur," said Stacey.

"Yuck," said Polly.

"Cool," said Park.

"I wonder what he eats," said Jaws.

No one could recall ever having seen Basement Bart eat anything, either.

That kept them busy for the rest of lunch. Park got to say lots of gross things, and Polly got to shriek and frown. And everyone left Alex alone about the bathroom.

But he didn't stop thinking about it. What exactly had happened in there? Had he imagined the whole thing? Or was it some kind of evil trick? He eyed Bent across the lunchroom. But he didn't think Bent was behind it.

Alex's gaze went to Stacey and Maria and Polly. The girls? Would the girls do something like that?

He tried to imagine Polly in the boys' bathroom. He made a face. It was not a pretty picture.

But if it was some kind of joke, how had they done it?

The disgusting smell could have been easy to do. But that didn't explain what had happened later, when he'd gone back with Basement Bart. Everyone had been in class then. Plus, Basement Bart had been there. He would have found any joke that any student had rigged up. Alex was sure about that.

He remembered that Basement Bart hadn't even considered the possibility of its being a joke. He had just warned Alex to stay away from the bathroom.

The bell rang, and Alex stood up and picked up his tray and went to dump it, still pondering the problem. As he passed Bent's table, Bent suddenly said, "Hey, Alex! Flushed out any good smells lately?"

Everyone laughed.

Alex forced himself to smile.

But as he left the lunchroom, he decided he was going to do two very important things. One, he was going to follow Basement Bart's advice. He was going to stay out of the boys' bathroom on the first floor at the back of the school.

And two, he wasn't going to tell anybody about what had happened to him when he'd gone back to the bathroom with Basement Bart.

Let the claws come out of the smoke and grab someone else.

He hoped they grabbed Bentley first.

CHAPTER
4

Park Addams was in the boys' bathroom minding his own business when it happened.

He was in a hurry. The bell was about to ring. He wasn't even thinking about what Alex said had happened to him in the bathroom the day before.

The boys' bathroom on the first floor at the back of the school near the old graveyard just happened to be handy.

He charged in and checked out the stalls. A pair of feet in red sneakers was under the first stall door. No problem. He went into the other stall.

He closed the door.

Then he realized what he'd seen in the stall next to him. And remembered Alex and the Nose Bomb Incident.

Park shut his eyes. He sniffed cautiously.

Something smelled. A faint burning odor. Sort of like burgers on the grill. Except that the burgers would be rotten and burning.

A chill crept up Park's back. Slowly he opened his eyes. Slowly he bent down to peer under the wall that divided the two bathroom stalls.

The red sneakers were still there. They were half hidden behind a giant spiderweb. As Park watched, a shiny black spider dropped down and then climbed back up.

That was unsettling. But not really frightening. It wasn't the spider that made Park's mouth drop open and his eyes bulge out.

It was the shoes. And the socks. As Park watched, one of the toes of the shoes began to tap slowly.

Tap. Tap. Tap.

But there were no legs coming out of the shoes. Above the socks, which seemed to be standing up of their own accord, was nothing but thin air.

Park straightened up slowly. Slowly, quietly, he began to back out of the stall, never taking his eyes off the edge of the sneaker that was going *Tap. Tap. Tap.*

He'd gotten the stall door open when the sneaker stopped moving up and down.

Park froze.

One of the socks drooped slightly. Then something seemed to pull it back up into place. The smell of something rotten frying grew stronger and more disgusting.

Willing himself not to scream or run, Park took another step back.

Then the shoes shuffled forward.

The stall door next to Park began to swing slowly open.

With a sigh, Alex bent forward to study his locker. He was sure he'd left his science book in it that morning. But maybe he hadn't. Maybe he'd left it at home.

Had he? He opened his pack and peered inside and spotted the corner of his science book.

Sometimes I think my locker is haunted or something, thought Alex. *Like gremlins or something go in and rearrange everything when I'm not around.*

He had to grin. *Yeah,* he thought, *and that's why my room at home is never clean. I wonder if my parents would believe that? I wonder—*

Something hit him hard in the shoulder. Alex lost his balance and went sprawling into the middle of the hall. Polly, who had just started walking away from her locker nearby, shrieked as Alex skidded shoulder first into her ankles.

"*Eeek!* Quit trying to look up my skirt, Alex Lee!"

"Get a grip, Polly. You're not wearing a skirt," Alex said desperately. "Get a grip and get lost!"

"Hmmmph!" said Polly. She stuck her nose in the air and marched away. Still crashed on the hall floor, Alex watched her feet and ankles disappear. It was true. She wasn't wearing a skirt. She was wearing flowered tights, pink scrunch socks, and incredibly clean white sneakers.

"Get up!" Park grabbed Alex above his elbow and began to pull him to his feet.

"Hey!" Alex yanked his arm free and got to his knees, groping for the books, papers, and pencils that had spilled from his pack.

"We haven't got time for that," said Park. "It's an emergency!"

Ignoring Park, Alex kept on gathering up his books. He stuffed his science book securely down in the bottom of his pack. He crammed his notebook in. He threw his math book into his locker.

"Alex!"

Alex checked the floor. He checked his pack. He checked his locker. He slammed the locker door, zipped his pack, and stood up to face Park. "What?"

Park's face was pale. He was twitching. His brown hair stood up on his head as if he'd been shocked with an electric current.

"It's true," he said. "You were right."

Alex frowned. "What are you talking about?"

"The bathroom," said Park. He looked wildly around, as if he was afraid of being overheard. Then he leaned close to Alex and said, "There's something wrong with the bathroom. It stinks."

Disgusted with Park's feeble attempt at humor, Alex turned and started walking down the hall toward his science class.

"Wait! Alex! That's not all. I saw something. Something really weird."

Alex stopped. "Smoke?" he said. "A, um, person? Part of a person?" He was remembering the claw that had come out of the smoke the day before. Remembering? How could he forget?

Park caught up with Alex. "Part of a person? Interesting question, Alex." The panic that had rewired Park's brain was obviously subsiding, and Park was thinking clearly again. "Why would you think I saw a body part? Unless you'd—shhh! Here come Stacey and Maria! Act normal. Pretend nothing is wrong."

As the two girls walked by, Park gave them a wide, loony grin. Maria frowned. Stacey frowned.

"Is something wrong, Park?" asked Stacey.

"Wrong? No? What could be wrong?"

Stacey frowned harder.

"C'mon," said Maria. "We're going to be late." The two girls hurried by. Alex looked over his shoulder and saw that Stacey was looking suspiciously over hers.

"Very cool, Park," he said sarcastically.

But Park wasn't listening. He was staring at Alex intently. "Body parts," he said again. His eyes narrowed. "You know something about that bathroom that you're not telling, don't you, Alex?"

Alex and Park stared at each other. Then Park said, "Meet me by the downstairs back boys' bathroom after school. Or else."

The bell rang.

The school was dim and the halls were quiet. The echo of the last bell had died away. So had the sound of student feet, eagerly stampeding to freedom.

Alex was lurking. He was lurking outside the bathroom door. He'd dropped a Susan B. Anthony dollar in a corner of the hall. If anyone came along, he was going to say he'd dropped some money and was looking for it.

Where was Park? Alex was pretty sure he wasn't already in the bathroom. He pushed the door open. He called Park's name.

Was Park pulling some kind of dumb joke? Had Bent put him up to it? *Were* the girls in on it, too?

Alex walked to the end of the hall and stared out through the windows of heavy mesh-reinforced glass that made up the top halves of the school's back doors. The old graveyard that covered the hill behind the school looked peaceful in the slanting rays of the afternoon sun.

This corner of the school was the closest to the graveyard. It was a new section of the building that had been added on to make new classrooms when the library on the other side of the school had been expanded.

Alex squinted. Had something moved, up on top of Graveyard Hill? He'd heard stories, but—

Something grabbed his shoulder. Alex leaped into the air with a horrible, strangled shriek.

CHAPTER
5

"Shhhhhh!" hissed Park.

"Good grief, Alex!" said Stacey.

"*Eeeh* . . . What are *you* doing here?" Alex asked Stacey, stifling the scream and pretending he'd never meant to scream at all.

Park dragged them both into the corner by the water fountain. "Shhh!"

They were silent.

The building was silent.

Park leaned out and looked all around. He leaned back in.

"What?" whispered Alex. "What're you looking for?"

"I almost got caught by Basement Bart once in the school one afternoon after everyone had left," said Park very, very softly. "I don't want it to happen again."

"What?" Alex said again.

"Long story. Later," said Park. He leaned out again to peer down the hall. He seemed satisfied with what he saw. Or didn't see. "Let's go."

"Go? Go where?"

Park pointed down the hall in the direction of the boys' bathroom.

"No. No way!" Alex folded his arms and glared at Park. "I'm not going in there ever again."

Park folded his arms and glared back. "I knew it! I knew you were holding out on me!"

Stacey stepped out in front of Park and Alex and glared at them both. "Would someone mind, please, telling me exactly what is going on here?"

"What I want to know is, what are you doing here?" Alex said. "What's she doing here?" he said to Park.

"Witness," said Park. "We need an impartial witness."

"Witness to what?" demanded Stacey.

Park looked from Alex to Stacey and then back to Alex. "You tell her, Alex. And while you're at it, tell me, too."

Alex opened his mouth.

A soft, horrible groan filled their corner of the hall.

Stacey jumped back, her eyes wide. "How did you do that?" she demanded. "Is this some kind of a joke?"

Alex closed his mouth. The groan sounded again—faint, but not very far away. A kind of buried-alive sound.

Park grew pale. Stacey gulped. Then she said, "Y-You're not a ventriloquist or anything, Alex? Are you?"

"No," said Alex with regret.

The groan sounded a third time. But this time it wasn't just a moan. Words were mixed in with the sound.

"Help meeeeeeee . . ."

The three students froze. Then, slowly, slowly, they turned their heads in the direction of the sound.

It was coming from the boys' bathroom.

Stacey was the first to react. "Someone's hurt!" she said. "Someone needs help! Come on!" She turned and ran toward the bathroom door.

"Stop her!" shouted Alex. "Don't let her go in there!"

"Don't be silly," said Stacey. "I don't care if it's the boys' bathroom. This is an emergency!"

"Stop!" howled Alex, forgetting to keep his voice down, forgetting to be afraid. He leaped across the hall with superhuman strength and grabbed Stacey by the back of her shirt just as she pushed on the door.

The door flew open at her touch. Smoke poured out. A huge, sucking roar filled the hall.

Stacey jerked forward as if she were attached to a rope being yanked into the bathroom.

Alex was jerked forward, too.

He pulled back with all his might. But no matter how

hard he pulled, the force from inside the bathroom pulled harder.

He and Stacey were being pulled inside. Smoke billowed around them.

Nasty hands, shaped like claws, reached out toward them both.

They were going to be—

Something hit Alex and Stacey and knocked them sideways. Alex's feet flew out from under him. He felt Stacey's shirt tear, but he held on.

Then he and Stacey and Park were sprawled in a heap to one side of the bathroom door as it slowly swung shut. They watched in disbelief as the smoke withdrew.

Then the hall was dark and still, as if nothing had ever happened.

Except for the faint smell of smoke.

Stacey sat up. She looked over her shoulder at the long strip of cloth dangling from her shirttail and from Alex's hand. "You can let go now," she said.

Alex let go of the torn shirt and sat up, too. Park, who had hit them both sideways with a flying tackle, got to his knees and shook his head as if to clear it. Then he looked at Alex.

"You had something you wanted to tell us about the boys' bathroom, Alex?" Park asked.

*   *   *

They rode their bicycles slowly away from the school.

Park kept looking over his shoulder. "I can't believe Basement Bart didn't hear us," he said.

"Maybe he did," Stacey said. "Maybe he heard us screaming for help and that's why he didn't come."

Alex didn't say anything. But he was thinking about what Basement Bart had said. *I'd stay out of that bathroom, if I was you.*

Did Basement Bart know something they didn't know? Was he behind this whole thing? Maybe there was buried treasure in the bathroom and Basement Bart knew it and he was trying to scare them away until he could find it and dig it up. . . .

Nah. That was like some dumb little-kid story. Buried treasure. No, there had to be a logical explanation for all this.

"There has to be a logical explanation for all this," said Alex aloud.

Stacey stopped her bicycle. She started to laugh. It was a shaky laugh. A mirthless laugh. An almost mean laugh.

"Logical?" she said. "Logical?" Graveyard School was almost out of sight behind them. But they could see its outline below, against the tombstone-strewn hill.

With a sweeping gesture of her arm, Stacey indicated the school, the playground, and the graveyard. "Logical?" she said for the third time. "I don't think so, Alex. Since when has there ever been a logical explanation for anything that's happened at Graveyard School?"

No one had an answer for that. The three of them turned and rode slowly on. By unspoken agreement, they didn't discuss what had happened until the school was safely out of sight.

Then Stacey said, "So what happened to you, Alex, in the boys' bathroom yesterday?"

Trying to sound calm and logical, even if the story wasn't, Alex told Stacey and Park about his second visit to the bathroom. He told them about getting trapped inside. About the icy cold, the frozen door, the fingers reaching out from the smoke.

He told them what Basement Bart had said.

Park, with equal calm, told about seeing the legless sneakers in the next stall.

"I think it's safe to say," Park concluded, "that there is something very, very wrong with that bathroom."

"Duh," said Stacey. But her expression was serious. Alex and Park could tell she was worried because she didn't make a single gross bathroom joke.

They were silent for a moment. No one wanted to say it aloud. Finally Alex did.

"You know it's true, don't you? That bathroom's haunted. There's a ghost in the boys' bathroom."

CHAPTER
6

"This is crazy," said Stacey. "Ghosts don't haunt bathrooms."

"So it's a crazy ghost," said Alex.

"That just makes it worse," said Park, trying to sound cool.

They'd reached Alex's house. His older brother, Michael, was shooting hoops with some friends in the driveway. He could see his little sister, Jenny, and her best friend up in the tree in the front yard and knew they were playing spy. Dinnertime was coming. Homework. Ordinary things.

Not crazy things. Not ghosts.

Why would a ghost haunt a bathroom?

"Why would a ghost haunt a bathroom?" asked Park, as if he could read Alex's mind.

"Maybe it died in there, like poor old dead Elvis," said Stacey.

Park and Alex were both startled. "What are you talking about?" asked Park.

"Elvis Presley. He died in the bathroom. That's where they found him," said Stacey.

"Forget Elvis," said Alex. "He's not haunting our bathroom." He paused. "At least I hope he isn't." He'd seen old Elvis movies on television.

Park and Stacey clearly had, too. They both nodded solemnly.

Then Alex went on. "If it's not Elvis, then who is it? I mean, does it have to be someone who"—he swallowed hard—"died there?"

"I think so," said Stacey. "I think that's a rule for being a ghost."

Another alarming thought struck Alex. "Do you think it was a kid?"

Both Stacey and Park looked shocked. Then Park said, slowly, "Well, it's mostly kids who use that bathroom. But what do you, I mean, what could happen to you in the bathroom?"

"Ex-Lax attack!" said Stacey.

No one laughed.

Not even Stacey.

"Sorry, guys," she said.

They all considered the idea of a kid buying it in the boys' bathroom. And how it might have happened. It wasn't a nice thought.

"What a way to go," muttered Park. "I mean, no matter how you picture it, doing the bathroom croak is—"

"Park, please," said Stacey.

Basement Bart's words came back to, well, haunt Alex once more. He felt a chill that was like a little sister of the icy air that had engulfed him when he'd been trapped behind the frozen bathroom door.

"Basement Bart," he whispered softly. "Maybe it was Basement Bart. . . ."

"Hey! Alex! What're you doing in there?" Alex's older brother slammed his fist against the bathroom door.

Alex jumped a mile. "Wh-What?"

"Hey! You've been in there twenty minutes. Don't you think you're taking this wash your hands for dinner thing a little too seriously?" Michael went on.

Looking down, Alex realized that he was still holding the soap from the bathroom sink in one hand. His mother had told him to wash his hands for dinner, but he still hadn't gotten around to it.

"We're hungry," warned Michael, his voice fading away. "This is the last call for dinner, soap-sucker."

"I'm not a . . . ," Alex began to protest automatically. But his voice trailed off.

Had something moved in the mirror? He spun around.

Blue-and-white tiles, navy towels, a blue-and-white-striped shower curtain, a navy bathmat. A white toilet, a white sink, a white bathtub. An ordinary bathroom.

The toilet gurgled. Alex jumped again. Then he froze. What if something was hiding under the closed seat of the toilet? What if . . .

Slowly he reached out for the lid. His hand hovered above it.

You're being the wonderwimp of the world, he told himself. *Get real. Get a grip.*

You don't really believe in ghosts, do you?

His fingers tightened on the lid.

At that moment the toilet gurgled again. And above the sink the bathroom cabinet door, which had a bad catch, flew open.

"Aaah!" shouted Alex. The soap squirted out of his hand. He shot out of the bathroom. He was tearing into the kitchen full speed before he realized that nothing had happened.

That it was all in his imagination.

His father handed him a bowl of carrots and pointed through the door toward the dining room table. "Dinner is served," he announced, and followed Alex to the table, where Alex's mother, sister, and brother sat.

His mother gave him a slightly worried look. "Are you okay, Alex?" she asked. "You're not feeling sick or anything, are you?"

"No!" said Alex hastily. He slid into his seat. He cleared his throat. He said, as casually as he could, "By the way, has anybody ever, you know, like, ah, *died* in our bathroom?"

"I can't believe you did that!" exclaimed Park. "I can't believe you actually asked your parents that! What did they say?"

Alex shrugged. "My brother started laughing. So did my mom and dad. Then Dad said he hoped not, since we bought the house brand new. Then my mother said something about me watching too much television and playing too many weird video games, so I dropped it."

"Smart move." Park turned to look over his shoulder. He and Alex and Stacey were standing on the steps of the school, where all the students congregated each morning before the first bell. By unwritten rule, the lowly first-graders were at the bottom, the sixth-graders were at the top, and all the other grades were in order, more or less, on the steps in between.

Dr. Morthouse or Hannibal Lucre, the oozy assistant principal, was also probably nearby. Students who had the stomach for it so early in the morning could peer through the thick, narrow glass panels in the doors and spot a figure lurking on the other side, maybe catch a gleam of light from Dr. Morthouse's silver tooth or the bald spot beneath the thin strands of hair combed across Mr. Lucre's head.

Sometimes the teachers used the front entrance, walking through the students as if they weren't there. But mostly they used the back entrance.

Does Basement Bart only use the basement entrance? Alex wondered.

"Basement Bart," he said aloud.

A gloomy silence fell.

The night before, they'd all realized that they had to face the awful truth.

There *was* a ghost in the boys' bathroom.

And Basement Bart was somehow involved.

Stacey had said flatly, "I'm not going to go ask Basement Bart any questions."

"Why not?" Alex had said. "You're in this, too."

She shook her head. "No, I'm not. I mean, okay, yeah, you've got a ghost problem. But it's in the *boys'* bathroom. Not the girls'."

"Hey, if it was in the girls' bathroom, I'd be there," said Park. But he didn't sound sincere.

And he and Stacey and Alex knew it.

Stacey gave Park a look. "I'll help," she said. "But I'm not going to talk to Basement Bart. And I think you'll agree that is the next step."

"Geez," Park said now. "Couldn't we just do some research first? I mean, we could, like, look him up in the newspapers or something. Check the crime section."

"Where do we go to look that up?" said Alex.

David Pike, a sixth-grader who was good at science

42

and who had a little brother who was a dinosaur freak, walked by as Alex spoke.

"Library," he said out of the corner of his mouth, as if he were giving out secret information.

"Huh?" said Alex, surprised.

"You want to look something up, go to the Grove Hill Library," said David. He added, "Or the school library maybe, but it's not as big."

"The library!" said Alex almost joyfully. "Thanks, David!"

David gave Alex a funny look and kept going.

Turning to Park, Alex said, "We can't use the school library anyway. What if Basement Bart found out? So that's what we'll do first. Right after school today, we'll go to the library and look up Basement Bart."

As the bell began to ring, Park nodded with enthusiasm and barely disguised relief. Until they'd checked things out at the library, they wouldn't have to talk to the janitor.

Now all they had to do was stay out of the bathroom.

"Newspapers?" the really tall librarian behind the front desk asked. "Some are on computer and some are in the basement waiting to be input."

"The basement?" said Park weakly.

She nodded and gave Park a friendly, slightly puzzled smile. "They're all indexed, of course. So you can look up the subject you're studying in the index and find out what issues of the newspaper covered it. If it's not listed

43

for any of the newspapers in the basement, then you won't have to go there."

"Right," said Alex. He pulled Park to one side for a quick conference. "How far back should we go?"

"Hmmm." Park thought for a minute. "Well, unless Basement Bart was a student at Graveyard School, maybe we should—"

"How do we know he wasn't a student there?" asked Alex. "How do we know that, ah, it didn't happen then?"

Park tried to imagine the janitor as a student. He couldn't. But Alex had a point. "Okay. We go back to as old as Basement Bart is."

"How old is that?" asked Alex.

Park shrugged. They both thought hard. Then Alex turned to face the librarian. "We need to go back at least, ah, sixty years—"

"Sixty!" interrupted Park. "He's not that old. . . ."

Alex dug his elbow into Park's side. "Sixty years," he said.

The librarian nodded as if Alex wasn't asking for anything unusual. "Log on to that computer on the table over there, type in *periodicals*—that means magazines and newspapers—and then you can break it down by subject and by the name of the magazine or newspaper, as well. Instructions are posted next to the computer, and it will tell you what to do, too."

"Thanks," said Alex.

"She's a nice librarian," said Park. "Too bad she's not at our school library."

"Forget about the school library," said Alex. "We've got work to do."

But there was no such person as Mr. Bartholomew (whose first name neither Park nor Alex could remember ever having heard) listed in any of the back issues of the Grove Hill newspaper, no reports of children mysteriously missing—or worse—from the school (or the school's bathrooms). Nor did Mr. Bartholomew's name turn up in any phone books or census reports or anything else that the librarian suggested they check.

It was creepy.

It was hopeless.

As they clicked off the computer, they knew it couldn't be avoided.

Basement Bart knew something. And the only way to find out what was to go and talk to him.

Alex was going to have to go back to the basement.

CHAPTER
7

The little kid went by so fast he was a blur.

Until Dr. Morthouse's long arm reached out and caught his own skinny one.

"Running in the hall," she said in her flat, cold voice.

The kid's feet kept moving for a minute, like a dog on a slippery floor trying to stop before it crashed.

Then he went limp.

Alex could see that he was just an ordinary little kid: scruffy jeans, sneakers with one shoelace untied, a rugby shirt decorated with playground dirt from morning recess.

The only thing unusual about him was that his olive-brown skin had gone green. And his brown eyes were wide with shock.

Dr. Morthouse didn't seem to notice. She said again, "Running in the hall is *dangerous*."

Seeming to sense that he was in real danger now that he was in Dr. Morthouse's clutches, the little kid swallowed hard. He blinked once. His eyes became slightly more focused. "Dangerous?" he said. He looked over his shoulder.

"And against the rules," the principal went on. "Unless, of course, you have a good reason. Like an emergency."

The kid craned his neck, staring back down the hall.

It was the downstairs hall. The one leading to the boys' bathroom.

Alex looked, too. The hall was empty.

He sniffed.

Almost empty. Except for that smell. . . .

"Well?" said Dr. Morthouse. "Is there an emergency?"

The kid looked at Dr. Morthouse. He looked down the hall toward the bathroom. He opened his mouth.

Dr. Morthouse smiled.

The kid closed his mouth. He shook his head hopelessly. He mumbled something and Alex caught the words *bathroom* and *late to class* and *sorry*.

"Late to class?" said the principal. "Well. I tell you

48

what. I'll just *walk* you to class to make sure you get there on time.''

The kid, who'd been recovering his normal color, went green again. But he put up no fight as Dr. Morthouse marched him down the hall.

When the principal was out of sight, Alex forced himself to move in the direction of the boys' bathroom.

The hall was strangely empty. The rotten burning smell got stronger and stronger as Alex got closer and closer. At last he stopped, a safe ten feet from the door of the bathroom.

From inside the bathroom came a rumbling sound that reminded him of the belches he'd heard in the toilet at his house—only this was much, much louder and more menacing.

The door of the bathroom was glowing a faint red, the color of an ember on a barbecue grill.

And from under the door, tiny fingers of smoke were curling along the floor. Actual fingers that were snaking out toward him, *tap, tap, tap*ping, reaching for his feet. . . .

Alex stomped at the horrible groping fingers just once. He felt something tug at his foot.

He turned and ran for his life.

"Now!" he gasped. "Now!"

Park said, "Chill, Alex. We can't go now. It's lunchtime.''

"Forget lunch." Alex took a deep breath and pulled Park to one side of the lunchroom door. "Whatever's in the bathroom almost made lunch of a little kid just now."

That got Park's attention. "What?"

Quickly Alex told Park about the little kid, who had obviously come from the haunted bathroom. "I don't know what he saw," said Alex, "but you can tell that something's wrong standing ten feet from the bathroom door. I mean, the door glows, the insides rumble, and there's smoke in the hall."

"Not that Dr. Morthouse noticed," said Park.

"Nah. She was just happy she had a little kid to wax. But if we don't do something fast, the next little kid who goes in there isn't going to come out."

"Okay, okay." Park began to follow Alex. "Lunch looked pretty strange today anyway." He made a face. "I knew there was something wrong with it because Jaws kept saying how delicious it was."

The door of the basement was closed. It opened all too easily.

"You first," said Park. "You know the way."

"Wimp," said Alex without much enthusiasm.

"Yeah," Park answered, refusing to be baited.

Alex led the way down the steep stone steps into the dim pit of light carved out of the darkness.

"This is a major creepshow," muttered Park, walking so close behind Alex that he kept stepping on Alex's heels.

"Back off," said Alex. "There's his office."

This time the door was completely closed. The red-lettered KEEP OUT sign was the only color in the near dark that surrounded them.

"He's not here," said Park. "Let's go." He turned. Alex grabbed a handful of sweater and yanked backward.

"Okay. Let's stay," said Park.

"Mr. Bartholomew?" said Alex, as he had before.

As before, no one answered.

Park glanced around. "Remember in *Tom Sawyer* how he got lost in the caves and—"

"This isn't a book," said Alex grouchily. "And we're not going to get lost down here. . . . Mr. Bartholomew!"

A sudden single mocking echo brought his voice back to him from one of the tunnels.

Or was it an echo?

"Mr. Bartholomew," mocked a hoarse, seldom-used-sounding voice from the tunnel of darkness to their left.

"That's not an echo," said Park.

A pair of Timberlands shuffled into the dim circle of light outside the janitor's door.

"Aaaaaaaah!" screamed Park. "It's the shoes! The haunted shoes!"

But it wasn't.

It was Basement Bart.

He turned his dark glasses on Park, and Park's scream

died in his throat. He gulped. "Uh, hello, Basement, uh, Mr. Bartholomew."

"Hi!" added Alex, trying to sound friendly.

The janitor didn't answer.

Park said, "Alex has some questions he'd like to ask you."

Alex decided that if he got out of this alive, he was going to turn Park into ghost material.

Basement Bart still didn't speak. He just stood there, waiting. Massive. Mean-looking. With all the dark tunnels of the basement behind him.

The silence grew. And grew. The basement didn't make any of the usual basement noises. No pipes clanked. No furnaces murmured. It was a dark, sound-proof world.

Maybe Basement Bart had been down there so long that the light hurt his eyes. Maybe he could only see in the dark. Maybe that was why he wore dark glasses.

Park said, "Alex. Go on. Ask your questions."

"Right," said Alex. He gave the janitor his best smile.

"Don't smile," said the janitor.

Alex wiped the smile off his face.

"Talk or walk," said the janitor.

"Right," repeated Alex. Where to begin? He took a deep breath. "Mr. Bartholomew," he blurted out, "if a kid had been, say, killed, like, you know, by accident, in, say, the boys' bathroom on the first floor, you wouldn't know anything about it. Would you?"

Park jerked his head around to look at Alex in alarm. "Are you crazy?"

Not the right question, thought Alex. *Okay. That's okay.*

He opened his mouth to try again.

But he didn't get a chance. Because a terrible, terrible sound was coming out of Basement Bart's mouth.

In spite of himself, Alex took a step backward.

Park groaned as if he was in pain.

The janitor bent forward and slapped his knees.

And kept on laughing.

CHAPTER
8

"Let's get out of here," Park said in Alex's ear. "Before he stops laughing and starts carving . . ."

But Alex had had enough. "Excuse me," he said.

Basement Bart kept on laughing. His mouth opened and closed. That sound came out.

"Excuse me," said Alex again, his voice getting louder.

"Come *on*," Park whispered.

"Excuse me, Mr. Bartholomew. Could you stop laughing and give us some help here?" said Alex.

As abruptly as he had begun, Basement Bart ceased to be amused. He straightened up. He turned a blank face toward Alex.

Behind Alex, Park made a strangled sound.

Basement Bart kept his dark glasses trained on Alex. Alex tried to make himself look fierce and determined, instead of smaller than the janitor and much more terrified.

Basement Bart said, in an almost conversational tone, "Are any kids missing?"

"N-No," said Alex.

"Interesting idea, though," said Basement Bart.

"No!" Park burst out.

The three of them were silent. To Alex's surprise, Basement Bart was the first one to speak. "What makes you think something happened to a kid in that bathroom?"

"Well," said Alex, and stopped, stumped again. It was all too weird. Way too weird.

"Go on, Alex, tell him," urged Park.

The dark glasses turned from Alex to Park and back to Alex. "Alex, huh," said the janitor.

Great, thought Alex. *Now he knows my name.*

Aloud he said, "Thanks, Park."

The janitor's lips moved in what might have been a smile. "And Park," he added.

Another stifled sound came from Park. Now Alex and Park were even. Alex felt better. More courageous.

He took a deep breath. "Park and I think that bathroom is haunted," he said. "We figure that if it is, it's because some kid, you know, uh, passed on in there. And his ghost is haunting the bathroom.''

What had Alex expected? That Basement Bart would confess? Laugh his unearthly laugh again? Chase them up the basement stairs and down the halls?

The janitor shook his head. ''Nope.''

Again they waited. Then Park said, ''Nope? What do you mean, nope?''

''Nothing like that ever happened in that bathroom.''

''Right,'' said Alex. ''It's the pipes.''

But Basement Bart was unmoved by Alex's sarcasm. ''Nope,'' he said again.

''Nope?'' echoed Park. He was clearly feeling braver.

''Bathroom's practically brand new. They redid the whole thing after that . . . earthquake.''

This was true. That was why everyone called it the new bathroom.

But it wasn't new, was it? It had always been there.

So why was the ghost haunting it now?

Alex looked up to find the dark glasses focusing on him again.

''You know something, don't you?'' he blurted out. ''You know that bathroom is haunted. I bet you even know why.''

''So?'' Basement Bart reached up and gave the overhead light chain a yank.

The basement went from dim to dark.

''Hey!'' shouted Alex.

His voice echoed down the tunnels.

Alex stuck out his hands like a sleepwalker. They met nothing but dark air.

Then his hand hit something. Alex screamed.

Park screamed. Park hit Alex.

Alex socked Park back. "It's me!" he shouted.

"Owww!" said Park. Then, "Oh."

"Mr. Bartholomew?" called Alex. The echo came back a mocking stammer. Alex couldn't tell if it was an echo, or the janitor.

"Mr. Bartholomew!"

The echo came back, faint and fading. They were alone in the darkness in the basement.

Alone with the rats. And the bats. And whatever else lived in the tunnels or crawled down from the graveyard. What did bony feet sound like, walking through the darkness? Did the joints of skeletons click and pop as they walked? Or did they move as silently as . . .

Ghosts?

A breath of cold air brushed Alex's cheek. His whole body was suddenly damp and cold.

The ghost, he thought. *It's the ghost! It's come back to get us!*

He spun around and crashed into Park again. "We have to get out of here!" he shouted.

Park said, "Don't panic."

"I'm not!" Alex shouted.

Something howled from the depths of the basement. Something inhuman. Something hungry.

"Me either!" shouted Park.

They both began to scream.

They were screaming so loudly that they didn't notice it at first: a dim crack of light, widening in the air above them.

Then Alex stopped screaming and pointed upward. "L-Look," he whispered hoarsely. Realizing that Park couldn't see, he reached out and grabbed a handful of shirt. "Look!"

Park stopped screaming. Then he saw it, too.

The door at the top of the steep, narrow basement steps was slowly swinging open. In the widening crack of light, they could see the outline of the upper steps.

"Let's go!" said Alex, bounding forward.

"Wait!" Now Park grabbed Alex's shirt, pulling him back.

"Why?"

"What if it's a trick?"

That stopped Alex. He turned. In the dim light Alex could see Park's pale face and staring eyes.

"It's not a trick," he said. "Let's get out of here."

But Park was frozen in place. And he had Alex's shirt in a monster-tight grip. Alex pulled. Park held on.

"Park, come *on*."

Park still didn't move. Except his lips. They twitched. ". . . Trick," he breathed.

Panic had frozen Park in place.

Then, to Alex's horror, he realized that the light was growing dimmer again. He turned. The door at the top of the stairs was slowly swinging shut.

He spun back around. He raised his arm and pointed past Park. *"Park!"* he shouted. *"Look out!"*

CHAPTER
9

Park let go of Alex. He streaked past him in a gray blur. A moment later he was pounding up the narrow steps toward the door with Alex on his heels. They shot out through the wedge of light and into the hall, and the door closed behind them with a heavy, final thunk.

Park didn't stop running until he reached the door of the lunchroom. There he bent over, trying to catch his breath. He looked sideways up at Alex.

"What was it," he panted, "a ghost?"

Alex shook his head, trying to catch his own breath.

"I'm not sure," he said at last. He'd never tell Park the truth. That his shout was nothing except a desperate attempt on his part to get Park unfrozen and moving again.

Whatever had howled in that basement would howl again, and trick or no trick, Alex hadn't wanted to be around when it happened.

"The ghost," said Park in a more normal tone of voice. He straightened up. "There is a ghost, you know. Basement Bart knows it, too. He didn't even act surprised."

Alex nodded. They walked slowly into the lunchroom. Although it seemed as if they had been gone for hours, students in their lunch period were still in the cafeteria line. Most of them were still eating.

"Basement Bart knows something," Alex said. "But he's not going to tell us. He doesn't care if the bathroom is haunted. That just means less work for him."

"Until the ghost starts bagging kids for real," said Park. "That's gonna make an awful mess."

"We have to stop it before then," said Alex. He remembered the frozen door, the bony fingers made of smoke reaching out for him. He shuddered.

They had to stop the ghost, and soon.

But how?

"Hey, ghostbusteroos," said Stacey, sitting down next to them.

Park continued to smush his Jell-O into his mashed potatoes without answering. Alex nodded.

"Bad, huh?" said Stacey sympathetically.

"We went to see Basement Bart," said Alex.

Stacey's eyes widened. "For real? Again? What happened?"

Cheering up a little, Park began to tell the story. He made it sound even scarier than it was, Alex thought. If that was possible.

"And something chased us all the way back to the lunchroom door."

"Wow. Decent cool," said Stacey, impressed.

"Yeah, but it doesn't help us any. We already knew Basement Bart wasn't wrapped right. Big surprise," said Alex bitterly.

Stacey said, "Well, he did give you a clue, at least."

"Clue? What clue? What're you talking about?" demanded Alex.

Opening her eyes wide, Stacey said, "You mean you didn't get it?"

"I was busy trying to stay alive," said Park sarcastically. He gave Stacey an evil look.

Stacey stuck her tongue out at him.

"What clue?" Alex practically shouted.

Stacey smoothed back her long, brown braid and smiled smugly. "Just that the bathroom is new. Practically brand new. Since the earthquake." She made a face as she said the word *earthquake*. None of the kids really believed that an earthquake had trashed the school not so long ago. Most kids thought it was something much bigger—and much weirder.

But whatever it was, the bathroom had been totaled, along with the whole back entrance of the school, rows of lockers, and at least one classroom.

Alex thought fast. "Oh," he said, "that. I thought you meant a real clue."

But Stacey wasn't fooled. "You hadn't thought of it, had you, Alex?"

"Thought of what?" asked Park.

Quickly, before Stacey could answer, Alex said, "That the bathroom wasn't haunted before the repairs were made. The old bathroom wasn't haunted. But the new one is."

Park frowned. Then he said, "So that means the ghost is connected to the earthquake?"

"Or to the repairs," said Stacey.

"What? They hired a plumber who installs haunted toilets?" Park cracked up at his own wit. "Flush! Boo!"

Alex didn't laugh. Neither did Stacey. "Shhh," said Stacey. "Here comes Polly Hannah."

Holding her nose in the air and her tray at a perfect ninety-degree angle to her perfectly upright body, Polly stopped beside their table. "I hope you're satisfied," she said to Alex.

"Actually, lunch wasn't that bad," said Alex.

"Not that," Polly said scornfully. "I mean the rumors you started about the boys' bathroom."

"What rumors?" Alex asked, although he knew what was coming.

"That it's haunted. None of the little kids will go near it. Maria told me her sister, who's in the first grade, says that none of the first-graders will even use the back door by the boys' bathroom, except at recess when the teacher is with them."

"I didn't start any rumors," said Alex.

"Hah," said Polly. She started to walk away. Then she added, "Wait'll Dr. Morthouse finds out. You're going to get it."

She was gone before Alex could answer.

"If Dr. Morthouse finds out, you *are* gonna get it," said Park solemnly. "Polly's disgusting, but she's telling the truth."

"Me? What about you? You're in this, too! And so are you, Stacey! Who almost got flushed backward into that bathroom? Who tried to save you?"

"Gotta go," said Stacey, grabbing her tray and jumping to her feet.

"Traitor!" shouted Alex. "Coward!"

Stacey gave Alex a pitying look. "In case you haven't noticed, Alex Lee, I don't use the boys' bathroom. Never have, never will. But if you need any more help with the clues, feel free to give me a call."

Then she walked away, too.

"Girls," said Alex in disgust.

Park said, "She has a point."

65

"Thanks. First you agree with Polly, and now with Stacey. Whose side are you on?" Alex glared at Park.

Wisely, Park decided to keep quiet.

They finished lunch in silence.

It was only when they were walking out of the lunchroom that Park offered Alex his final opinion.

"Alex?"

"What?"

"We have to find out who built the new bathroom."

Hearing Park's words, Alex had a bad feeling. A very bad feeling.

"Yeah," he agreed cautiously.

"There's only one way to find out."

Alex looked at Park. Park looked at Alex.

Then Park said, "The principal's office."

The phone rang twice. The second time, a familiar, sour voice answered. "Grove Hill Elementary School. This is Mr. Kinderbane speaking."

Alex cleared his throat and tried to speak in a low voice. "Hello. I understand the school had some repair work done on it recently."

Mr. Kinderbane's voice grew sourer. "Correct."

"I was wondering if you could tell me who did the plumbing repairs."

"Who is this?" said Mr. Kinderbane.

"Alexander," said Alex, without thinking. Then he added, "Mr. Alexander."

66

"Alex Lee, is that you?" said Mr. Kinderbane.

"Uh," said Alex.

"I don't have time for these stupid tricks."

"It's not a trick!" yelped Alex. "It's important. Really important! It's . . . it's for a school project."

"Hah," said Mr. Kinderbane. Then he said, "It's no big secret. Deep Six Plumbers." He hung up the phone.

Alex stared at the receiver. "Wow. He just told me. Like it was no big deal. Deep Six Plumbers."

"Deep Six Plumbers? What kind of a name is that?" asked Park.

Hanging up the phone, Alex said, "I don't know. But I bet they're the only plumbers by that name in the phone book."

He was right. All the other plumbers listed in the yellow pages had ordinary names. Deep Six stood alone.

Literally. It was in an old house at the edge of the downtown district of Grove Hill. An old claw-footed bathtub had been filled with dirt and plants and put in the front yard. As Alex and Park rode up on their bicycles, the gleam of chrome and porcelain flashed from the big bay window downstairs.

Leaning their bicycles against a tree, they walked up the worn front steps. The chrome and porcelain proved to be a plumbing supply display in the window. When they walked in, they discovered that the whole front room was filled with toilets and bathtubs and a wall of faucets and showerheads and hot and cold spigots.

67

"Cool," said Park, examining a bright green toilet with the words ENVIRONMENTALLY EFFICIENT!!!! written on a sign hung from its handle.

"Need some help?" a voice asked.

Park and Alex turned to face a large man who looked, for a moment, frighteningly like Basement Bart.

Alex gave a little gasp.

Then he realized that he must have been imagining things. This guy was as big as the school janitor, and he had long hair pulled back in a ponytail. But he was mostly bald. And he was wearing overalls and a T-shirt that had once been white. The front of the overalls stretched out over a beachball stomach, and the guy had little round eyes in a face that was as round as his stomach. A mustache drooped like a horseshoe around his mouth and chin.

"Well?" said the man.

"Are you the plumber?" asked Park.

"Yeah. Ralph Smith."

"Did you do the plumbing for Grove Hill Elementary School after the earthquake?" asked Alex.

The plumber's round eyes got smaller. "Yeah. Why?"

"We just wondered, you know. About how it was done." Alex thought fast and came up with the same old reason. "For a report. For school. Jobs people do. So we chose plumbing and then Mr. Kinderbane told us you—"

"Oh. Mr. Kinderbane." For some reason the name of

the sour Graveyard School secretary seemed to reassure the plumber. "Yeah. A school report, eh? Well, now's as good a time as any to give you a little interview." The plumber sat down on the closed lid of a display toilet and motioned for Park and Alex to sit on two others. "I first decided I wanted to be a plumber when I was eleven and the upstairs bathroom flooded. I . . ." He paused and frowned at the two boys. "Aren't you going to take notes?"

"Notes?" asked Alex.

"You said it was a report, dincha?"

"Oh. Right." Hastily Alex dug into his backpack and produced a notebook and pen.

Mr. Smith began to talk. Alex began to write. And write. And write.

Every time he or Park tried to ask a question about the plumbing job at Graveyard School, Mr. Smith said, "I'll get to that," and kept on talking.

Alex felt as if he were in a class from the dark side.

At last Mr. Smith stopped. He cleared his throat. "That's when I got the Grove Hill School job," he said. "Biggest challenge of my career. School budgets are always small, y'know. People expect their kids to get educated, but they don't want to pay for it. Well, you get what you pay for, is what I say."

"The bathroom?" Park reminded Mr. Smith. "The boys' bathroom?"

"Yeah. A mess. A total wipeout. Someone had to

come in and build it from the ground up." He shook his head. "And get this. Big-shot contractor, he put the bathroom in the wrong place!"

Both Alex and Park were startled. "The wrong place," said Alex. "But the bathroom's where it has always been."

Mr. Smith shook his head and grinned triumphantly. "Nope. You just think it is."

"What do you mean?" asked Park.

"That bathroom's a good six, seven feet to the left of where it was before. I had to lay in new pipe, completely redesign the bathroom. A mess. A mess."

Alex said, "You mean the bathroom's not where it was before?"

"Not entirely. Six feet of it, maybe more, is on brand-new ground. Your principal made the contractor come back in and build that nice brick planter there, underneath the bathroom window outside, to hide the fact that the building's lopsided now." He added proudly, "That was my idea."

"Could we see the design for the new bathroom?"

"The blueprint? Sure. I kept it. I use it to impress new clients." The plumber got up and walked bouncily out of the showroom. He returned a moment later, unrolling a big sheet of paper with an outline of Graveyard School drawn on it in blue. He pointed to a square at the back of the building. "The solid line is

70

where the new bathroom went. The dotted line is where the old one was."

Park and Alex examined the blueprint. It was hard to tell anything about the bathroom from it. But Alex asked, "Could we get a copy of this? For our report?"

"Sure thing," said Mr. Smith. "Got a copier right here in my office."

A short time later, Alex and Park were waving good-bye to Mr. Smith. Alex had a copy of the blueprint tucked safely in his backpack.

They had another clue. But as far as Alex could see, they were no closer to getting rid of the ghost in the boys' bathroom than they had been before.

CHAPTER
10

Five A.M.

Alex groaned and closed his eyes and tried to go back to sleep.

Something gurgled. He put his hand over his stomach. *Breakfast is hours away,* he told it silently. *Don't wake up now.*

The gurgle came again. The sound wasn't coming from his stomach.

Alex sat up. Little eddies of water were swirling around the four legs of his bed. One of his shoes was rocking, as gently as a toy boat, on a shallow sea that filled his bedroom. The other shoe was sinking, toe down.

He saw it all in one wild glance, by the pale early-morning light filtering through his window.

It's not possible, thought Alex. *I live on the second floor.*

Leaping out of bed, he landed with a splash in the middle of his room. The water was icy cold. He waded to the window to look out, expecting to see a flood, a sea, surging and roiling just below his window.

The street was peaceful and still. The streetlamp on the corner spotlighted the neatly swept curb, the smooth, white sidewalk, a carefully trimmed hedge, the rough bark of a tree.

The night was bone dry—at least outside Alex's window.

Carefully Alex stepped back from the window. He looked down again at the lake in his room.

It was ebbing away. Sliding out beneath the closed door of his room. He could feel the water pulling on his pajama legs like the undertow at the beach.

Alex's heart began to pound. He didn't like the look of this. It gave him a bad feeling.

Then he thought, *It's probably a broken pipe. I should go tell someone.*

Feeling less uneasy, Alex waded across the room. His door opened against the tide of water with some difficulty, but at last he was able to step out into the hall.

A dark river of water was flowing away from him toward the bathroom. A sense of relief washed over Alex.

It was a broken pipe after all. Nothing to worry about—unless the leak had anything to do with the toilet. Alex wrinkled his nose and waded forward.

Not until he began to push the bathroom door open did he realize what was wrong with the picture.

If the pipe in the bathroom was broken, the water should be running out of the bathroom—not back into it.

Quickly Alex tried to jerk the bathroom door shut.

But he was too late.

His hand suddenly seemed stuck to the doorknob. The door flung itself open and jerked Alex into the dark bathroom. A swell of water rushed past him.

The toilet lid lifted like the upper lip of some nightmare animal. The sound that came out as the water was sucked back into it wasn't nice.

It was laughter.

Alex screamed. He leaped back. His feet slipped out from under him and he landed with a splash. Waves rose above him and slapped the bathroom walls high above his head, only to come crashing back down on him.

He tried to scream again, then thought better of opening his mouth while it was at water level. He got to his hands and knees, and a wave struck him from behind. He belly-flopped forward, making even more waves.

The laughter grew louder.

And then Alex smelled it: the rotten, burning smell.

With clumsy desperation, he began to thrash along the floor of the bathroom toward the dark outline of the door.

Something grabbed his leg. In spite of himself, he screamed again.

The light went on.

"Alex! What's going on in here?"

Blinking in the sudden brightness, Alex stared up at his brother, Michael.

"I don't know," Alex managed to answer at last.

A voice spoke in the hall behind Michael. He turned and answered. "It's okay, Mom. It's just Alex, goofing."

His mother raised her voice. "Go to bed now," she said in her warning tone. Then her voice faded as she went back down the hall, calling reassurances to Alex's father. Alex heard his name repeated and what might have been a chuckle from his father.

But it was not a laughing matter.

Alex raised his gaze to Michael. He pushed back the wet hair plastered on his forehead.

"I'm not goofing," Alex said.

"You call taking a shower with your pajamas on in the middle of the night in the dark not goofing?" asked his brother.

"I wasn't taking a shower. The shower's not even on!" said Alex.

For a moment Michael's voice grew more serious.

"You didn't hurt yourself when you slipped as you got out, did you? Hit your head?"

"No!" Alex shouted.

"Chill," said Michael, then paused. Then he added, "Which is what you're gonna do if you don't get some dry jams on. Come on."

Why won't he let me explain? Alex thought.

Then he looked around the bathroom. No water dripped down the walls. No reverse-running river spread out from the lip of the toilet. The lid was closed, and no sound came from it.

The bathroom was dry as a bone. The only wet thing in it was Alex, sprawled in a sodden heap on the floor.

"Come on," repeated Michael. He stepped back and motioned through the open bathroom door.

Alex gave up. At least he wasn't going to drown in toilet water in his bathroom. That would have been truly gross. At least now he was getting out alive.

Quickly Alex got to his feet. He leaped for the open door and through it.

Michael shook his head and rolled his eyes and turned back down the hall toward his room.

Back in his own room, Alex took off his pajamas and put his clothes on, just in case. Then he stuffed the soggy pajamas under his door to keep out any rising tides that might invade the house.

Finally he climbed back up on his bed to wait.

*   *   *

"You look bad. Washed out," said Jaws. "Aren't you getting enough to eat?"

Ignoring Jaws, Alex reached out and grabbed the ball in midair, right before Park could catch it.

"Hey!" protested Park. "I've got to practice. It'll be baseball season in—"

"Later," said Alex. He threw the ball to Jaws. "Play ball."

Alex steered Park a safe distance away from the others on the playground.

Park eyed Alex uneasily. "You do look kinda kicked," he said.

"I had a bad night," said Alex. "A haunted one, you might say."

"Excuse me?" said Park, his voice getting sharp.

"You heard me. The ghost followed me home. It turned up in the bathroom at our house."

"What?" said Park.

"It flooded the bathroom and tried to drown me. I think it thought it was funny." Alex remembered the evil gurgling laughter spilling from the toilet and shuddered. "We've got to figure out what's going on and why. And we've got to stop this ghost before it's too late."

"We've already agreed to that," said Park. Alex could tell that Park once again was trying to be cool. And once again he was failing.

Miserably.

"How do you stop a ghost?" Park said.

"You have to lay it to rest, or something, don't you?" said Alex. He stopped. He frowned. "Lay it to rest . . . but what's upset it? Like, how can you make a ghost chill if you don't even know why it's haunting something?"

"I don't know," said Park. "But I'm not about to go in the bathroom and ask it."

Alex said, "Park. You're a genius."

"No I'm not," said Park instantly.

"It's brilliant!"

"No it isn't," said Park.

Ignoring him, Alex said, "That's exactly what we have to do. We have to go and ask the ghost what the problem is. And when we find out, then maybe we can fix it."

"No. *N.O.* Big *No.* Not me. I'm not going in there and saying, like, 'Excuse me, Ghost, but before you drown me in toilet water and burn me alive and freeze me to stone, could you please tell me why you're so upset?' "

"We'll just talk to it," Alex said. "Reason with it."

Park said, "Have you been hanging out in the guidance counselor's office or something? *Talk* to it?"

"Why not? You got a better idea?"

Park turned to go. Suddenly, with a strength he hadn't known he possessed, Alex grabbed Park's arm and yanked him back.

·"Hey!" said Park.

"You're in this with me, Parker. I'm not going back into that bathroom alone. You're coming with me."

"No," said Park feebly.

Alex let go of Park's arm. "Fine. I'll go talk to the ghost by myself. Don't worry about me. But if I go into that bathroom and never come out, don't forget to tell my parents what happened . . . chicken."

With that Alex turned and walked away, in search of a teacher who would give him a bathroom pass.

CHAPTER
11

He stood alone in the dark hall. The door of the boys' bathroom was closed.

It looked like an ordinary door.

Maybe we've been imagining all this, thought Alex. *Maybe we've imagined everything. Stranger things have happened at Graveyard School.*

He glanced through the window panels in the back doors of the school, toward the old graveyard.

What a creepshow! He didn't even like to think about what was buried up there. Things that weren't human, probably.

Things that liked to stroll down the hill and haunt the bathroom when they got bored?

Nah.

Maybe.

He took a step toward the door. Then another one.

The hall stayed quiet. The door stayed closed. Just an ordinary door.

Then he saw it. The OUT OF ORDER sign on the door.

Basement Bart had been there. That's why they hadn't heard anything else about weird happenings in the bathroom. No one had been going in.

Alex wondered if that made the ghost angry.

He swallowed hard. He took another step forward. And another.

He had just reached the door and put his hand on it when he looked down and saw it.

Water.

A thin trickle of water was inching out from beneath the door and curling around the soles of his shoes.

For a moment his mind went blank with panic. For a moment he almost ran.

But somehow he managed not to. Somehow he managed to push the bathroom door open and walk inside.

It's the middle of the day, he told himself. *What can happen?*

"Alex!" the voice whispered, and Alex nearly catapulted backward through the door in shock before he realized who had spoken. Park was pressed against the wall just inside the bathroom door.

"Park! What are you doing here?"

Holding up his bathroom pass, Park said, "Where have you been? You're late!"

Alex pulled his pack off his shoulder and swung it around so that Park could see it. "I went by my locker to get some tools. Just in case."

Park glanced around toward the bathroom, and so did Alex.

Nothing.

Alex looked down.

The floor was dry.

So was his mouth. But he managed not to let his hands shake too badly as he opened the pack to reveal what he had brought.

"A plunger?" said Park in disbelief. "Drain opener?"

"Not the chemical kind. This one is like an air gun. It shoots air down the drain to unclog it," Alex said. "It's not dangerous or anything."

But Park was holding up the giant pipe wrench. He gave Alex an amazed look.

"It's a pipe wrench," Alex explained. "My father uses it when he works on the plumbing."

"This is pitiful," said Park. "We've come to talk to a ghost and you've brought plumbing supplies. It's almost enough to make me laugh."

"Don't say that!"

But it was too late. As if the ghost had been waiting for a cue, it made its entrance.

A horrible, gurgling laughter began to bubble up out of all the toilets in the bathroom.

Park had never heard that sound before. It broke his nerve completely. He charged for the door.

He threw his shoulder against it. "Owww!" He fell back, rubbing his shoulder hard. "It's stuck."

Alex barely glanced at the door. "Not stuck. Frozen."

Park stuck out his hand to touch the handle and jerked it back. "It *is* frozen."

Never taking his eyes off the flapping toilet lids and the stall doors, which had suddenly begun to slam open and shut, Alex thrust his pack at Park. "Something to melt the ice."

Then he walked boldly forward into the middle of the room.

The toilets clamped shut. The stall doors slammed and were still.

Alex said, "Uh, hello."

Behind him he heard Park say, "A blow-dryer!"

"Uh, we'd like to talk to you."

The smell of something rotten and burning filled the bathroom so suddenly and so strongly that it brought tears to Alex's eyes. He tried not to breathe through his nose.

"We'd like to, uh, know why you're so upset. Why you've started haunting this bathroom. We want to help."

A geyser of water suddenly shot up from one of the sinks. The smell of burning grew stronger.

"Couldn't you at least think about it?" Alex said.

The geyser stopped. The bathroom grew absolutely still.

Alex waited. Park waited.

Nothing happened.

Finally Park said, "This door is still frozen shut. I'm gonna plug this hair dryer in and blast it." He went toward an outlet just inside the bathroom door, holding the plug of the dryer in his hand.

Alex barely managed to stop Park in time. "Park, no! It's a trick."

"What? Why?"

Wordlessly Alex pointed down at the thin sheet of water that had suddenly spread across the bathroom door. Then he pointed to the tag on the blow-dryer that said DANGER: ELECTRIC SHOCK; DO NOT USE NEAR WATER.

"If you plug it in, we fry."

The pale green of the bathroom walls was reflected in Park's face. Hastily he dropped the blow-dryer back into Alex's backpack.

Somewhere a bell rang.

Recess was over. Everyone else was going back to class. For once in his life, Alex wished that he was, too. He wanted to be anywhere but where he was: trapped in a bathroom with a ghost.

Alex stepped farther out into the bathroom. "Hey,"

he said. "Can't we be friends here? Don't you think you're being a little bit unreasonable?"

It was a phrase Alex's father was fond of using whenever he was trying to make Alex do something Alex had complained about.

For that reason alone, Alex should have known it wouldn't work.

Park said, "I think we could make it through those windows."

Instantly the windows froze over.

"Good going, Park," said Alex out of the side of his mouth. In a louder, friendlier tone he said, "We just want to talk."

Instantly all the toilet lids and stall doors began to slam up and down and back and forth again. The insane noise did sound a little like a crazy conversation. But it wasn't exactly helpful.

Putting his hands over his ears, Alex shouted, *"Stop that!"*

To his surprise, the noise stopped.

"Ask it to open the door," urged Park in a soft voice.

"Not right now," said Alex quickly, afraid the ghost would take offense. "I think we've established a connection."

He said to the bathroom, "Who are you? Why are you here?"

"Alex."

"Shhh . . . C'mon, trust us. Talk to us."

"Alex."

"What?"

Park said, "Look." He pointed.

Alex looked. And although the bathroom was frozen shut, he felt sweat break out on his forehead.

Tiny red beads were appearing on the walls and rolling slowly down them.

"Blood," said Park.

"It's not!" said Alex. "It's a ghost trick. Ignore it."

At that instant he became aware that they were not alone in the bathroom. Beneath the stall door on the far end of the row, a pair of sneakers was materializing.

"Them. That's them!" said Park, pointing at the sneakers.

The sneakers stood there for a moment. Then they shuffled forward. The stall door flew open. The sneakers stepped out. One of the toes began to tap up and down. Up and down.

Tap, tap, tap, tap.

An ominous echo joined the tapping. The faucets had all begun to drip in time. The walls were oozing red. But the faucets were dripping yellow slime.

"We've gotta get out of here," said Park. "Alex? Time to g-g—"

Without warning, the shoes broke into a run. They ran straight for Alex and Park.

CHAPTER

12

"Runnnnnnnnn!" shouted Park.

But it was too late. The shoes were upon them. They began to kick furiously at Alex's legs—hard, sharp blows, as if the toes of the sneakers were made of steel.

"Owwww!" Alex jumped back, trying to dodge the furiously kicking feet. When he turned, the sneakers kicked him in the ankles, the backs of the knees. They ran up his back and kicked him between the shoulders.

"Park! Help!" Alex shouted, ducking as the toe of one sneaker whistled past his ear. The sneaker tumbled off his shoulder and he swung at it. He caught it on the heel and sent it flying against a wall.

Something whistled past his other ear and he ducked instinctively. The other sneaker flew through the air, hit the mirror, and fell into the sink.

Alex turned. Park had the plunger held over his head like a sword.

"Get a weapon!" he shouted.

Alex dove for the bag as the two sneakers left their respective positions and began to run toward each other.

Alex seized the pipe wrench. He whirled and brought it down hard on the first sneaker, shattering the tile floor with the blow.

A horrible scream split the air. Molten yellow gunk began to bubble furiously up out of the sinks. The other shoe kicked the wastebasket like a football into the air. It went into end-over-end orbit around the room, spewing garbage.

Smoke boiled up out of nowhere, filling the room with the horrible smell of burning rotten meat.

Park suction-cupped the other sneaker against the wall with the plunger. "Gotcha!" he shouted.

The toilet lids all flew open, and geysers of toilet water shot into the air.

The shoe under the pipe wrench wriggled free.

Alex leaped forward and landed on it with both feet. It gave a tremendous kick, and he lost his balance. He swung wildly at it again, and the force of the blow spiderwebbed the floor with a huge crack.

"Help!" shouted Park. The sneaker stuck in the suction cup of the plunger was hopping around the room, dragging Park with it, rolling him in the red goo on the walls, dipping him in the foul yellow ooze that was boiling out of the sinks.

The smoke grew thicker and thicker. Hardly knowing what he was doing, Alex chased the sneaker across the bathroom, swinging wildly as he went. He dented metal doors. Cracked walls. Knocked a toilet lid into orbit with the rest of the garbage.

Then he realized, as he passed under Park, who was being hopscotched along the ceiling, that the walls and ceiling were cracking and breaking.

The sneaker shot out from under the next stall and booted him on the knee.

Manic laughter echoed hollowly around the walls.

"I think . . . you made it . . . mad . . . ," gasped Park, raising his feet to push off one of the frozen windows and trying to wrench the sneaker-clogged suction cup at the end of the plunger handle free from a wall.

It wasn't just mad. It was having the biggest of all ghost temper tantrums.

Alex had never thought about what could be scarier than a ghost. Now he realized what it was—a ghost who was angry with him, personally.

The shoe got him in the shin, and he swung without thinking and almost hit himself in the leg. Wicked laughter howled around him as the shoe skipped away.

The cracks widened. Foul-smelling smoke poured out

of them, and the drops of red and globs of yellow sizzled against the walls and floor.

The whole floor began to buckle. Alex slipped and slid, fighting to keep his balance. The shoe danced around him gleefully, darting in for nasty kicks at every opportunity.

The shoe in the plunger began to whirl Park around in circles. Hanging on to the other end, Park swung helplessly above the bathroom.

The wall at the far end of the bathroom crumbled with a mighty roar and fell backward. A jagged seam opened in the tile at the edge of the floor.

Park lost his grip on the wooden handle of the plunger and fell. He landed on Alex, and they both went down.

Alex wasn't quite sure what happened next. The impact of Park's fall knocked all the wind out of him. He remembered feeling the icy coldness of the floor under his hand, despite the smoke pouring around him.

Somewhere far away he heard the school fire alarm begin to sound.

The tiles under his hands crumbled like cereal. The snaking cracks in the floor and ceiling widened into yawns. Sinks fell from the walls. Toilets heaved into the air. Water spouted, and red and yellow slime oozed. The wastebasket continued its orbit above the room. Paper towels shot out of the towel dispenser and became big wet spit-and-goo balls.

A crack opened along the floor toward Park and Alex.

"We're going down!" shouted Alex.

He closed his eyes and prepared for the worst.

A huge, rumbling roar filled the air. The laughter grew louder and louder. Alex felt something give his leg one final vindictive kick.

The floor rolled like a swell on the ocean.

And then everything was horribly, absolutely silent.

Alex waited.

And waited.

Nothing happened. No sound except the distant shriek of the fire alarm and the random *splat* of debris falling off walls and other piles of debris.

Alex opened his eyes.

"Park?" he said.

Beside him, Park opened his eyes.

"Whoa," said Park.

The bathroom was totaled. The only clear space in the whole room was where Alex and Park had fallen. They could see the sky and the graveyard through the space where the wall had been.

It would have been a perfect view, except for one large object in the way.

Thrust up from the crevice where the wall had met the floor of the bathroom was a huge, ancient coffin.

CHAPTER
13

Alex and Park were heroes.

They left Graveyard School that day in an ambulance, although, as they both kept saying, they were just fine.

"Just fine," agreed the doctor at the hospital, and sent them home with their respective worried parents.

They had their pictures in the paper, next to the huge coffin that had appeared in the boys' bathroom.

By unspoken agreement, they didn't mention the haunting of the bathroom.

A building inspector came and checked over the site and said it looked as if the bathroom had collapsed because of a geological flaw, "an instability in the substructure of the earth."

The plumber was "surprised."

The plans for the bathroom were published, and it was established that the new bathroom had been moved slightly from the site of the old bathroom.

No one knew who the skeleton was in the coffin. But the coffin was identified by a local historian as of the same type as many of the others up in the old graveyard. No one knew why this particular coffin had been buried so far from the rest.

Dr. Morthouse issued a statement saying that the earthquake had shifted the coffin, which in turn had caused geological instability under the bathroom. After a careful evaluation, a new bathroom was being built—exactly on the site of the original bathroom.

The coffin and its ancient, brittle contents were taken up the hill and reburied where they were supposed to be, according to the town historian.

The earth closed quickly over the coffin, and in no time at all the grave looked just like all the others.

Because of certain rumors, when the new bathroom was completed Dr. Morthouse had a "Bathroom Opening Ceremony" during a special assembly. She cut a ribbon and made a speech praising the school, the plumber, the historian, the inspector, and Mr. Bartholomew. The glint of silver in her mouth, which many of the kids believed was a fang, gleamed repeatedly as she smiled and talked.

She didn't praise Alex or Park. If it hadn't been for the ambulance whisking them away to the emergency room after Basement Bart had found them amid the debris of the haunted bathroom, Alex suspected that Dr. Morthouse might have suspended them for life.

He was pretty sure she blamed them for the whole thing. The first (and only) thing she'd said as they were being led away to the ambulance was "Wasn't there an OUT OF ORDER sign posted on that bathroom?"

Alex and Park and Stacey stayed near the back of the crowd gathered in the hall.

"It wasn't geological instability, you know," said Stacey. "Those are just big words for 'I don't know what caused it.'" She shook her head in disgust. "As if it wasn't perfectly clear."

Alex said, "I know. They built the bathroom above a grave. That's what got the ghost going."

"Personally, I think the ghost was enjoying it all," said Park. "It got some pretty awesome special effects going."

"Walls that ooze red. Ugh," said Stacey.

"The smell was the worst thing," said Alex, remembering the expressions on the faces of the ambulance drivers and the nurses and doctors. They'd all thought the smell was basic bathroom gross.

But Alex—and Park—knew better.

Alex's mother had thrown his clothes away.

So had Park's.

Neither of them had protested. They knew that the smell wasn't ever coming out. It was an eternal bad smell.

Dr. Morthouse held up a pair of scissors that glinted with the same silver glint as the fang in her mouth. She cut the yellow ribbon across the bathroom door.

Assistant Principal Hannibal Lucre began to applaud. Others in the crowd, mostly teachers and little kids, joined in.

Alex and Park and Stacey didn't clap.

"What I don't get," said Alex, under cover of the applause, "is why that coffin was buried so far from all the others. I mean, you *know* it didn't slide down the hill during an earthquake 'cause you *know* we didn't *have* an earthquake."

Stacey nodded.

Park shrugged.

Alex said, "I mean, what if there was a reason this guy was buried so far away? I mean, maybe he was a troublemaker, or something. I mean, what if he wasn't bothered by the bathroom being built above him? What if it just meant he could escape? Become the ghost he wanted to be? I mean, maybe he wasn't angry after all. Maybe he was just mean."

Stacey and Park turned to look at Alex.

"Forget about it," said Park. "Some things are best left alone." He and Stacey exchanged a glance.

"Yeah," said Stacey. "It's over now. That's the main thing. Just forget it."

She and Park turned back to watch Dr. Morthouse. Things were back to normal. It was just another weird day at Graveyard School.

Something was behind Alex. The hair on the back of his neck stood up. He jumped up and spun around, backing against his locker.

Basement Bart stood there. He was holding something in one hand.

"Oh. Hi," said Alex.

"Found this," said the janitor. "Thought it might be yours." He thrust the object toward Alex. A smile of unearthly glee passed over his face.

Then he turned and walked away.

Alex looked down at what the janitor had pushed into his hand.

It was a plunger.

Attached to one end was a sneaker.

And as Alex stared at the sneaker caught in the end of the plunger, he was almost certain he saw the toe of the sneaker move up and down, up and down.

Tap, tap, tap.

Is your school haunted? Take this quick quiz and find out!

1. A typical noise in my classroom is:
   a. the drone of the teacher's voice
   b. the chatter of happy students
   c. a snore
   d. clanking chains and eerie moaning

2. In my school, one or more of the following objects has been known to disappear:
   a. pens and pencils
   b. the occasional mitten or gym sock
   c. bad report cards
   d. the entire fifth grade

3. Our janitor:
   a. keeps the floors spotless
   b. wears a spiffy uniform
   c. is friendly to teachers and students alike
   d. has no head

4. The new kid in our class:
   a. has really nice clothes
   b. seems shy, but will probably get over that
   c. moved here because her mother got transferred
   d. levitates and spins her head all the way around

5. Our classroom:
   a. has cheery posters on the walls
   b. is pretty boring
   c. has a guinea pig in a cage
   d. has cold spots and a hole in the floor where flames shoot out, usually during math

6. A typical school lunch includes:
   a. spaghetti and meatballs
   b. a bologna sandwich
   c. pizza
   d. tasty rat cutlet with creamy vomit sauce, side of cockroach salad

If you have answered (d) to one or more questions, run for your life! Your school is definitely haunted!

TILL YOU Laugh Scream!

With each and every one of these scary, creepy, delightfully, frightfully funny books, you'll be dying to go to the *Graveyard School!*

Order any or all of the books in this scary new series by **Tom B. Stone!** Just check off the titles you want, then fill out and mail the order form below.